Seven carefully selected Troll
stories from Icelandic folk tales
collected by Jón Árnason:

Trunt Trunt
Deep are the Ocean Trenches of Iceland
Gilitrutt
Grjótgarðsháls
An Earl's Daughter Captured by Trolls
Búkolla
Trolls of the West Fjords

Tales of Trolls

Icelandic folk tales collected by Jón Árnason

Adapted by Anna Kristín Ásbjörnsdóttir
Illustrated by Florence Helga Thibault

Trunt Trunt

There were once two men out in the mountains gathering herbs. One
night in the tent, one man slept peacefully while the other lay restless.
Suddenly, the sleeping man stood up and walked out of the tent. His
friend followed him and quickly realized that he was headed for the
glaciers. There, atop the glacier, sat a horrid ogress. She swung her arms to
and fro up to her chest, first one then the other, drawing the man towards
her. He ran straight into her arms, and they were soon gone.

A year later, the people from his village were travelling in the same place. The man appeared and barely uttered a word. They asked him what he believed in, to which he replied "God."

Two years later, he appeared once more to the people gathering herbs. He was now so troll-like that the people were afraid of him. He was again asked what he believed in, to which he did not reply, and quickly left.

Three years later, he appeared once again. He had grown into the most hideous and evil-looking troll. One man bravely asked him what he believed in, to which he replied "Trunt, Trunt and the trolls in the mountains!" and then disappeared. After that he was never seen again, for the villagers dared not go back to gather herbs there for many years after.

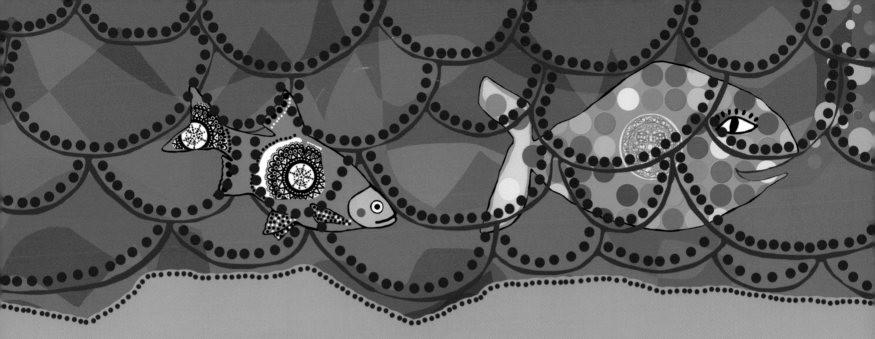

Deep are the Ocean Trenches of Iceland

There once was a ogress who wanted to wade across the sea from Norway to Iceland. But she had heard that there were deep ocean trenches in the sea floor along the way. Another ogress had warned her and advised her not to go, but she said "Deep are the ocean trenches of Iceland, but I will be able to wade across them."

She was told that one trench was so deep that the water would reach above her head. All the same, she set off for Iceland. When she reached the trench she so feared, she tried to grab onto a ship for support. But she lost her grip on the ship, tripped, plunged into the ocean and drowned.

Her body washed up at Rauðasandur. It was so gigantic that a man on a horse, reaching up with his whip, could not stretch high enough to reach her knee as she lay stiff and lifeless on the beach.

Gilitrutt

There once was a farmer under the Eyjafjöll Mountains. He was hard working, and had many sheep. The farmer was a newlywed when this story took place. His wife was young, but rather lazy and apathetic in her work. She couldn't be bothered to do anything, and did little around the farm. The farmer disliked this situation but could do little to change it. One autumn he gave his wife a lot of wool and asked her to spin and weave it over the wintertime. As winter passed, the wife never touched the wool, although her husband often reminded her.

   One day a craggy-featured old woman came to speak to the wife. She offered to spin the wool for her. All the young wife had to do was guess her name. The old woman said that she was allowed three guesses.

   The young wife accepted, and quickly handed her a large sack of wool. The old woman grabbed the sack and slung it onto her back saying "I will bring the woven cloth to you on the first day of summer," and went on her way.

   During the winter the farmer asked his wife often about the wool. The wife replied that it had nothing to do with him, and that he would receive the woven cloth on the first day of summer. The farmer didn't give it much thought and soon the last month of winter was upon them. The young wife began to wonder about the old hag's name, but couldn't think of any way to find it out. She grew increasingly worried and despondent. The farmer noticed this and asked what was the matter. The young wife then told her husband the whole story. The farmer was horror-struck, and told her that she had done a bad thing – that the old hag was most certainly a ogress who intended to take her away.

Shortly after, the farmer was walking under the mountain and came across a stony hillock. His mind was filled with his misfortune. Suddenly he heard a sound from the hill. As he approached it, he noticed a small gap in the rocks, and saw an old woman weaving at her loom. She held the loom between her legs, beating it as she chanted:

"Hey hey, ho ho! The housewife knows not my name! Hey hey ho ho! Gilitrutt is my name! Gilitrutt is my name! Hey hey, ho ho!"

The farmer was delighted and thought that this must be the hag who had tricked his wife. He hurried home and wrote down the name Gilitrutt. The last day of winter was upon them, and the farmer had not told his wife the name. The young wife was becoming more and more distraught, and did not get dressed that day. The farmer came to her and asked if she knew the ogress name. She said no, and that she would die of sorrow. The farmer said that wasn't necessary, because he knew her name. He went on to tell her how he came to hear it. The young woman trembled with fear; so afraid was she that the name might be wrong. She pleaded for her husband to stay by her side when the troll arrived. He refused, saying that she had got herself into this situation and it would be best that she resolve it herself. Then he left.

The first day of summer arrived, and the young woman lay in her bed, alone in the farmhouse. She heard a great rumbling as the ogress appeared, less friendly than before. She slung a great bolt of cloth onto the floor, and asked the young wife "What is my name?" The young woman was so afraid that she felt closer to death than life, and hesitantly guessed "Signý?"

"That is not my name, guess again young housewife."

"Ása?"

"That is not my name, guess again young housewife."

"I don't suppose your name is Gilitrutt?" asked the wife. The ogress was so stunned that she fell stiff as a board onto the floor with a loud thud. She then rose to her feet, walked away, and was never seen again.

The young wife was relieved that she had escaped from the ogress. After this incident she became hard-working and conscientious, and spun and wove all her wool herself.

Grjótgarðsháls

A long time ago, before Iceland was settled, two ogresses lived in the East. One lived by the sea and the other by the glacier. When they met one day, they began to quarrel about the land that lay between them, as both of them laid claim to it.

They agreed that they should both start walking with big strides, at the same time of day, one down by the sea and the other by the glacier. When they met they would mark the place. They met at a ridge in the southeast of the Möðrudalur estate, which was later named Grjótgarðsháls (Stonewall Ridge), after the stone wall they built to mark the boundary.

The boundary wall is one-and-a-half kilometres long and four to five fathoms high, built of huge rocks, up to two or three fathoms in diameter. The wall is much weathered now, but stands there to this day.

An Earl's Daughter Captured by Trolls

As was customary, some men from Skagafjörður went south to Suðurnes in late summer for the fishing season. They wanted to travel fast, so they went across the interior via the glaciers. But as they entered the upland wilderness they were caught in a blizzard and fog, so they lost their way. By dusk they arrived at large cliffs, where they found a cave in which they took shelter. There was enough space for their horses and their luggage. There they fed their horses, and ate as well. Whilst they were doing this a beautiful woman appeared. They asked her what her name was, to which she answered Ásgerður. They asked if she was alone, to which she replied that there were no other men there. They asked her why this was, to which she did not answer. Then she went away.

The next morning, the weather had improved, and so they decided to leave. The young woman appeared once more, but again said very little. But she accepted some food from the men. One of the group was an especially fine figure of a man. When they had gone a little way, he realised he had lost his knife, and went back to the cave to look for it.

The young woman asked what was the matter, and he said he was looking for his knife. She said that she was responsible, and handed him the knife. She said she had taken it so that she could talk to him alone.

"I am the daughter of an earl from Gotland. A troll and his ogress stole me from Sweden. They had a young son, to whom I was to be wed. I pleaded to be given

a year and a half before the wedding, but during that time the young troll grew ill and died. The troll couple were kind to me, and so I served them dutifully for some years, until the troll father fell ill and died too. I remained with the ogress, as I did not know where to go in this unknown land, and pitied her too much to leave her. She died shortly afterwards, and I have been here since. I ask you now to come back in the spring and take me away from here."

The young man promised to do so. When he headed north again in the spring, he looked for the cave and found the young woman. He took her down from the wilderness with her possessions – a great treasure. He exchanged the treasure for a good farm and then married Ásgerður, and they stayed together for the rest of their lives.

Búkolla

Once upon a time there were a man and his wife who lived in a cottage with their only son. They did not care for him much. The three of them lived there, with one cow named Búkolla. One day Búkolla went missing, and so both husband and wife went to look for her. They searched high and low for the cow, but could not find her. They became very angry and ordered their son to go out, and only return when he had found Búkolla. They sent him away with some food for the journey, and new shoes.

He walked for a long, long time until he finally sat down to eat a bite of his meal. As he sat down he said:

"Moo now, my Búkolla, if you are alive somewhere." At once he heard the sound of the cow from far, far away.

The young man began to walk towards the sound. He walked for a long, long time, until he sat down to eat a bite of his meal saying: "Moo now, my Búkolla, if you are alive somewhere." He heard the sound of the cow a little closer than before.

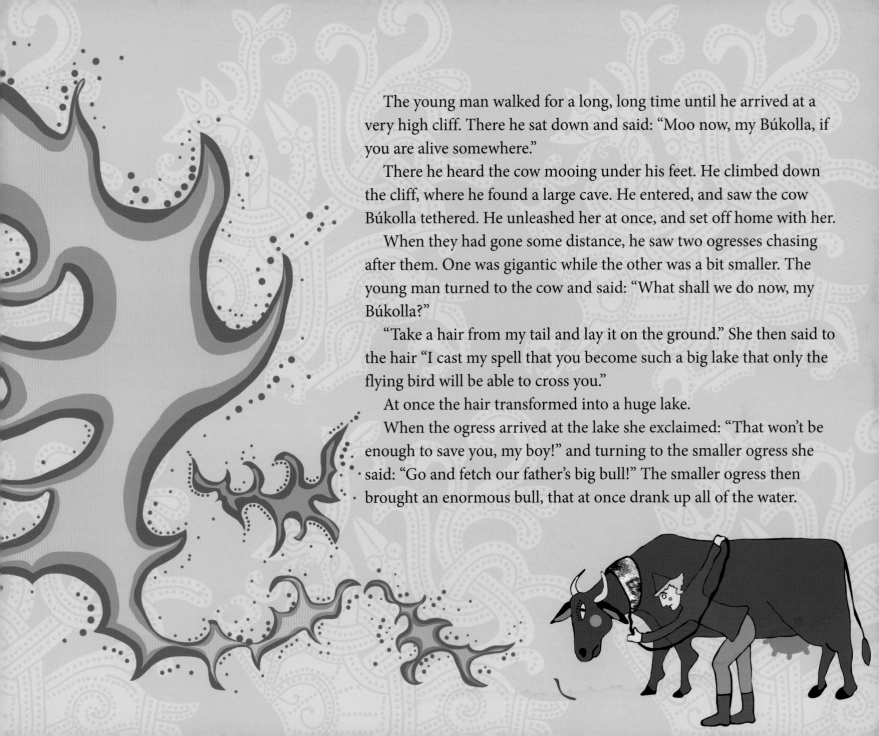

The young man walked for a long, long time until he arrived at a very high cliff. There he sat down and said: "Moo now, my Búkolla, if you are alive somewhere."

There he heard the cow mooing under his feet. He climbed down the cliff, where he found a large cave. He entered, and saw the cow Búkolla tethered. He unleashed her at once, and set off home with her.

When they had gone some distance, he saw two ogresses chasing after them. One was gigantic while the other was a bit smaller. The young man turned to the cow and said: "What shall we do now, my Búkolla?"

"Take a hair from my tail and lay it on the ground." She then said to the hair "I cast my spell that you become such a big lake that only the flying bird will be able to cross you."

At once the hair transformed into a huge lake.

When the ogress arrived at the lake she exclaimed: "That won't be enough to save you, my boy!" and turning to the smaller ogress she said: "Go and fetch our father's big bull!" The smaller ogress then brought an enormous bull, that at once drank up all of the water.

The young man saw that the ogress would catch him, as she ran with enormous strides. He turned to the cow and said: "What shall we do now, my Búkolla?"

"Take a hair from my tail and lay it on the ground." She then said to the hair "I cast my spell that you become such an immense fire that only the flying bird will be able to cross you." At once, the hair transformed into an immense fire.

When the ogress arrived at the fire she exclaimed: "That won't be enough to save you, my boy!" and turning to the smaller ogress she said: "Go and fetch our father's big bull!" The smaller ogress brought the bull, who urinated on the fire and put it out. The young man saw that the ogress would catch him, as she ran with enormous strides. "What shall we do now, my Búkolla?"

"Take a hair from my tail and lay it on the ground." She then said to the hair "I cast my spell that you become such a huge mountain that only the flying bird will be able to cross you." At once, the hair transformed into a gigantic mountain.

When the ogress arrived at the mountain she exclaimed: "That won't be enough to save you, my boy!"and turning to the smaller ogress she said: "Go and fetch our father's big drill!"

The ogress returned with the drill. At once, the larger ogress began to drill a hole into the mountain, but as soon as she could see through she impatiently forced herself into the hole, and stuck fast there. When the sun rose the ogress turned to stone, and she remains there to this day.

The young man returned home with Búkolla, and was warmly welcomed by his parents.

Trolls of the West Fjords

A long time ago three trolls lived in the West. They decided to dig a channel between the West Fjords and the mainland. They were going to use the land they shovelled to make islands in the bays on either side.

The digging went very well in the West, as the fjord was shallower there, and there were two to do the job. As they dug the trolls scattered rock over Breiðafjörður bay to form the innumerable islands that are like blueberries on a pudding on the bay today.

However, things did not go so smoothly in the East. Not only was the ogress alone, but also Húnaflói bay was much deeper. Most of what she dug formed reefs in the bay.

The trolls worked all night long and did not notice the sun creeping up into the sky. The trolls in the west began to run away as fast as they could, over Steindalsheiði heath, and tried to hide in Kollafjörður. However, by the time they had reached the beach, the sun had risen and they were turned to stone. They stand side by side in Drangavík and are now called Drangar or Stone Pillars. One rock pillar is larger at the top and then gradually tapers downward; that is the man. The other is narrow at the top and broadens downwards resembling a stomach and thighs; that is the woman.

The ogress digging from the East was also late. She leapt over Steingrímsfjörður and was at Malarhorn when the sun rose. She was furious because she had only managed to make a few islets where birds could nest, and hidden reefs. She angrily thrust the shovel into the ground, which split, broke off the mainland and formed the island we now call Grímsey. That is the only big island that the ogress was able to create. And it is said that the rock layers on the isle are the same as at Malarhorn, so it must be from there.

At the east end of Grímsey island stands a rock shaped like a bull. It stands tall and is called Uxi, which means Ox. The tallest end of the rock is said to be the ox's horn. The ox is said to have belonged to the ogress; it stood on the patch of land that broke off to form Grímsey Island.

Since then no-one has ever tried to make any islands in Breiðafjörður or Húnaflói, nor to dig a channel separating the West Fjords from the rest of Iceland.

Tales of Trolls

Icelandic folk tales collected by Jón Árnason

Illustrations © Florence Helga Thibault

Adaptation © Anna Kristín Ásbjörnsdóttir

Translated by Anna Yates

Printed in Slovenia

ISBN: 978-9935-9057-4-1

NÝHÖFN

2015

www.nyhofnutgafa.is